THIS BLOOMSBURY BOOK

BELONGS TO

. . . .

For Leo the lion-hearted – A.J.B.

To Nick, Daniel and Alexander with lots of love . . .
and to Rucola, Miele and Isotta – very happy dogs! – B.V.

Bloomsbury Publishing, London, Berlin, New York and Sydney

First published in Great Britain in August 2012 by Bloomsbury Publishing Plc
50 Bedford Square, London, WC1B 3DP

Text copyright © Alan James Brown 2012
Illustrations copyright © Barbara Vagnozzi 2012

The moral rights of the author and illustrator have been asserted

Manufactured and supplied under licence from the Zoological Society of London

A CIP catalogue record for this book is available from the British Library

ISBN 978 1 4088 1844 2

Printed in China by Toppan Leefung Printing Ltd, Dongguan, Guangdong

1 3 5 7 9 10 8 6 4 2

www.bloomsbury.com

www.storiesfromthezoo.com

The Zoological Society of London (ZSL) is a charity that provides help for animals at home and worldwide. We also run ZSL London Zoo and ZSL Whipsnade Zoo.

By buying this book, you have helped us raise money to continue our work with animals around the world.

Find out more at **zsl.org**

Never Lie
on a Lion

Alan James Brown

Illustrated by Barbara Vagnozzi

BLOOMSBURY

LONDON BERLIN NEW YORK SYDNEY

Never enter the lair
of a grizzly bear.

Grrr!
Grrr!

Never share a cake
with a great big snake.

Gulp! Gulp!

But do run a mile from a crocodile.

Never creep behind a sheep.

Baaa!
Baaa!

Never dance a jig
with a pot-bellied pig.

Grunt! Grunt!

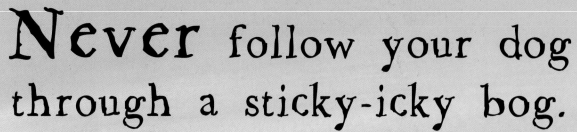

Never follow your dog
through a sticky-icky bog.

But do have a chat
with your cat.

Miaow!
Miaow!

Never race round a course chasing a horse.

Neigh! Neigh!

Never take a bow standing on a cow.

Moo! Moo!

Never try to put a whale
into a tiny little pail.

But when you see a monkey
Playing music that is funky,
Then join his friends as they
Do the funky monkey!

Toot! Toot!

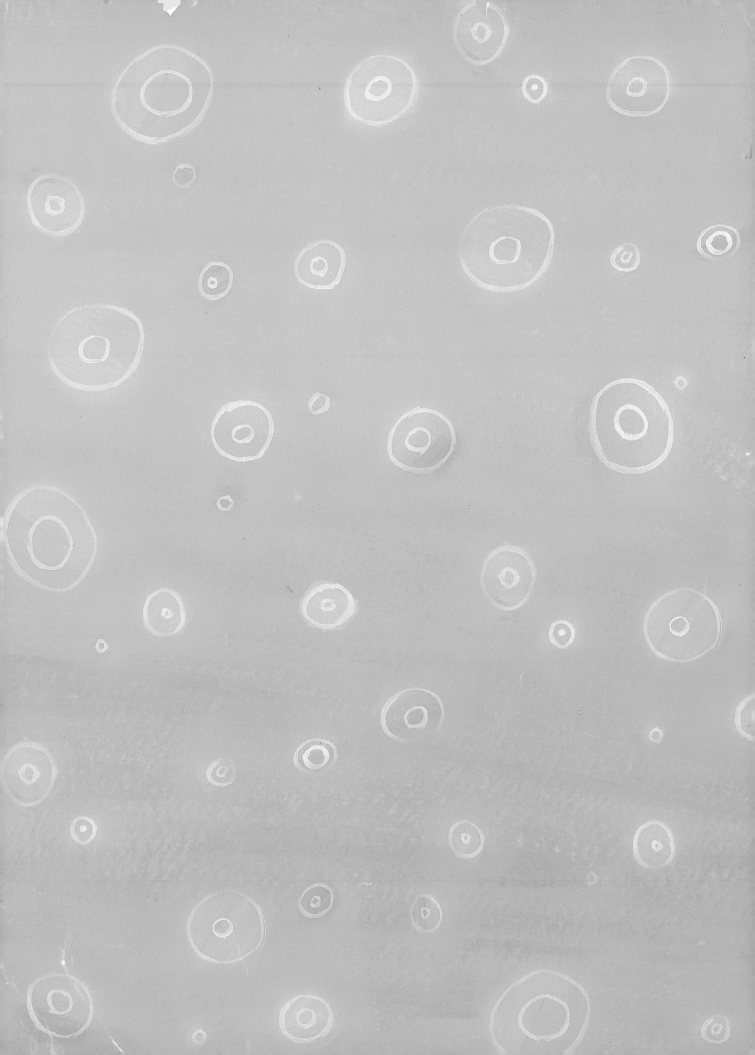

More fun-filled animal picture books . . . perfect for small paws!

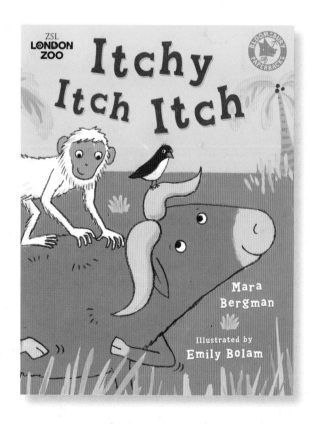

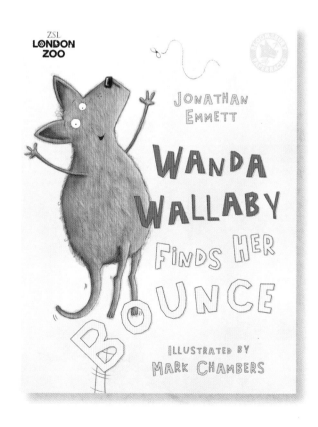

Visit www.storiesfromthezoo.com for exciting news, downloadable activity sheets, videos and much more!